This bo

Published by Ladybird Books Ltd
80 Strand London WC2R 0RL
A Penguin Company

19 20

Printed in Italy

Town Mouse and Country Mouse

illustrated by Jonathan Hateley

Ladybird

Once upon a time,
there were two mice.

Country Mouse lived
in the country.

Town Mouse lived
in the town.

One day, Town Mouse
went to see Country Mouse.

"What a funny house!"
said Town Mouse.
"What funny food!
What a funny bed!"

The two mice went for
a walk.

Suddenly, they heard
a noise:

Mooooooo!

"What's that?"
said Town Mouse.

"It's only a cow,"
said Country Mouse.

But Town Mouse was
very frightened.

Then they heard
another noise:

Hisssssssss!

"What's that?"
said Town Mouse.

"It's only a goose,"
said Country Mouse.

But Town Mouse was
very frightened.

Then they heard
another noise:

Whoooooooo!

"What's that?"
said Town Mouse.

"It's the owl,"
said Country Mouse.
"Run as fast as
you can!"

"I don't like it in
the country,"
said Town Mouse.
"Come with me
back to the town."
So off they went.

TO TOWN

17

"What a funny house,"
said Country Mouse.
"What funny food!
What a funny bed!"

The two mice went
for a walk.

Suddenly, they heard
a noise:

Parp Parp!

"What's that?"
said Country Mouse.

"It's only a car,"
said Town Mouse.

But Country Mouse
was very frightened.

Then they heard
another noise:

Wail!

"What's that?"
said Country Mouse.

"It's only a fire engine,"
said Town Mouse.

But Country Mouse
was very frightened.

Then they heard
another noise:

Meow!

"What's that?"
said Country Mouse.

"It's the cat!"
said Town Mouse.
"Run as fast as
you can!"

And Country Mouse ran
very fast—all the way
back to the country.

TO THE COUNTRY

Read It Yourself is a series of graded readers designed to give young children a confident and successful start to reading.

Level 2 is for children who are familiar with some simple words and can read short sentences. Each story in this level contains frequently repeated phrases which help children to read more fluently. Every page in the story is accompanied by a detailed illustration of the main action, which aids understanding of the text and encourages interest and enjoyment.

About this book

The story is told in a way which uses regular repetition of the main words and phrases. This enables children to recognise the words more and more easily as they progress through the book. An adult can help them to do this by pointing at the first letter of each word, and sometimes making the sound that the letter makes. Children will probably need less help as the story progresses.

Beginner readers need plenty of help and encouragement.